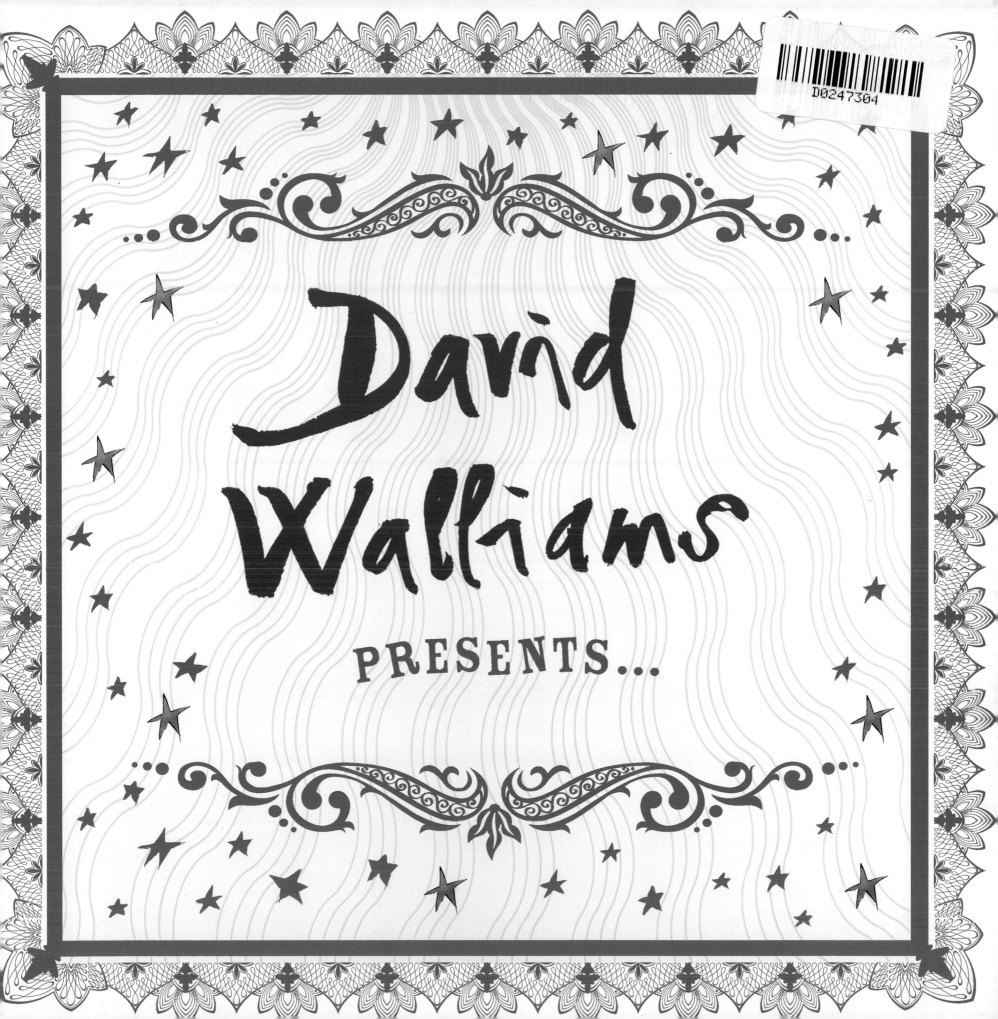

David Walliams

PRESENTS...

THE slightly ELE P

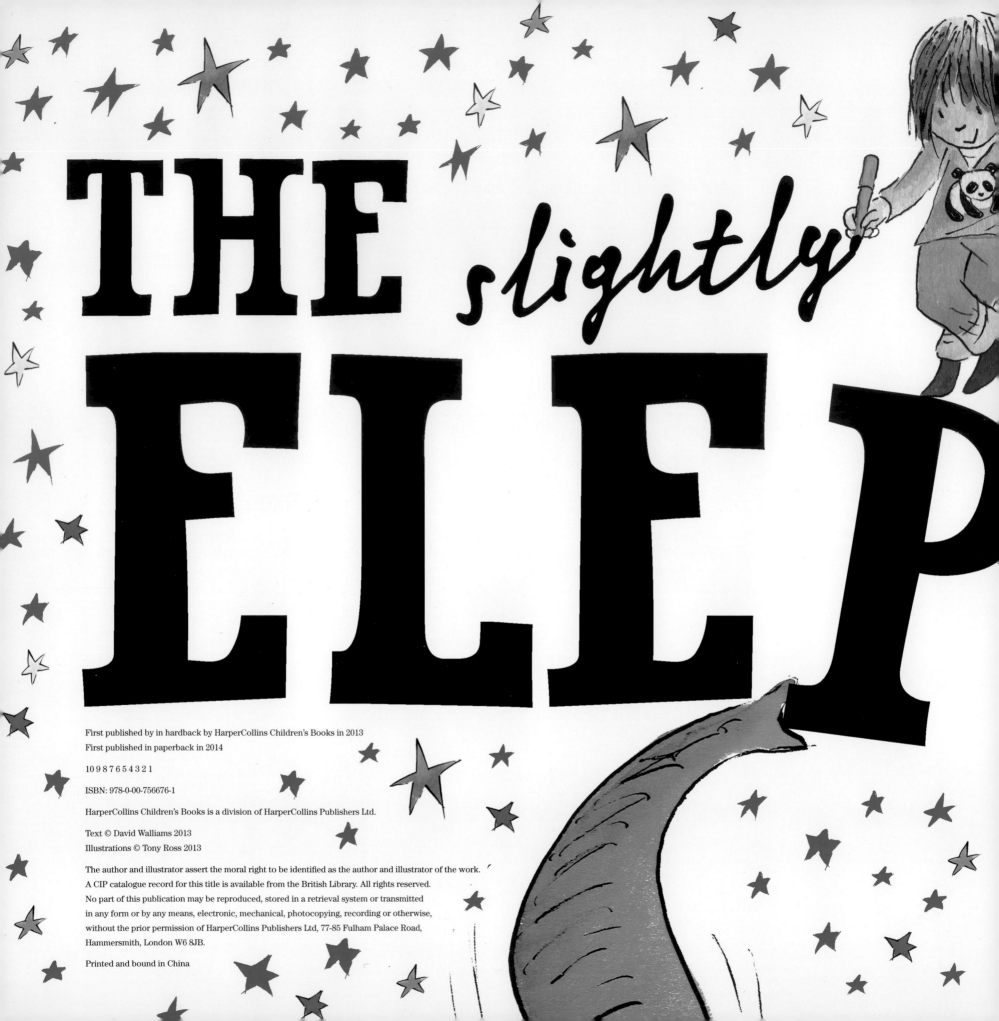

First published by in hardback by HarperCollins Children's Books in 2013

First published in paperback in 2014

10 9 8 7 6 5 4 3 2 1

ISBN: 978-0-00-756676-1

HarperCollins Children's Books is a division of HarperCollins Publishers Ltd.

Text © David Walliams 2013
Illustrations © Tony Ross 2013

Printed and bound in China

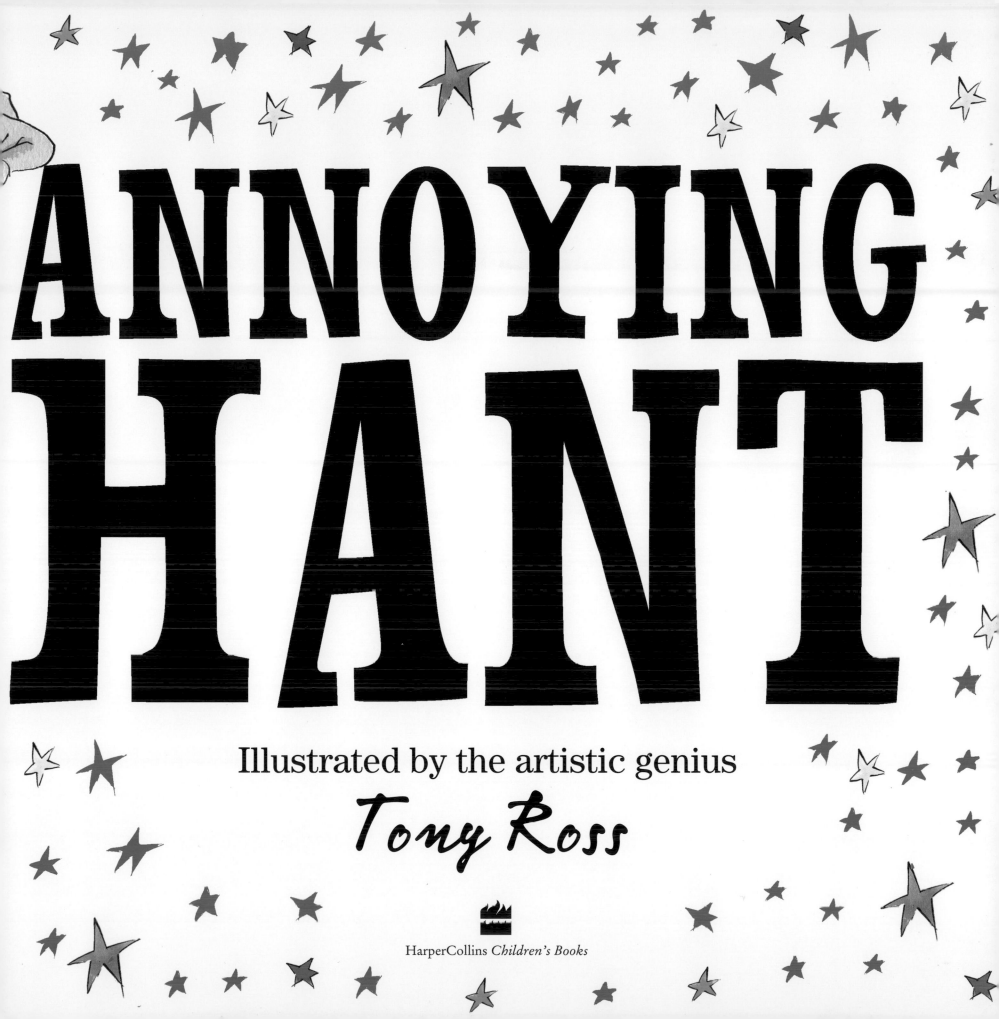

ANNOYING HANT

Illustrated by the artistic genius

Tony Ross

HarperCollins *Children's Books*

To Sam
and
Phoebe

D.W.

To
Jackson's
brother

T.R.

One day there was a loud knock
on the door. Sam ran down
the stairs to open it.
Was it his mum back
from the shops?
Was it a friend?
Was it the postman?

No...

It was an elephant.
A great, big, gigantic,
ginormous elephant.

"Hello Sam,"

he boomed.

"How do you know my name?" said Sam.

"You adopted me, don't YOU remember?"

"Well… I filled in an 'Adopt an Elephant' form at the zoo… but…" spluttered Sam.

The last thing he was expecting was the elephant to actually turn up on his doorstep.

"Now if you will excuse me, I need to take a bath," announced the elephant.

He pushed past Sam and made his way upstairs to the bathroom, knocking all the pictures off the walls as he went.

Because the elephant was so big all the water from the bath flooded the bathroom floor. What's more he used all the soap and all the towels. Instead of hanging the towels up afterwards, he left them strewn across the floor.

"**I am hungry,**" demanded the elephant.

"What do elephants eat?" asked Sam.

"**Food! Silly boy!**"

Sam sped into the kitchen and rummaged through the fridge and all of the cupboards. He poured all the food in the house into a massive pot and gave it a stir.

"Quickly, please!"

called the elephant from the living room.

As fast as he could, Sam raced into the living room where the elephant was sitting on Dad's armchair. Without a word the elephant dunked his trunk in the pot and slurped up all the food in one go.

"Now I have had my starter, what's the main course?"

he asked.

Later it was time for Sam's favourite cartoon to come on the television. The elephant was snoring loudly…

…and there was a boring show about antiques on. So Sam prised the remote control out of the elephant's foot and changed channels.

All of a sudden the elephant woke up.

"I was watching that!" he boomed.

"You were asleep!" protested Sam.

"I was not. I love shows about antiques."

"Oh, sorry. Do you collect antiques yourself?" asked Sam.

"Of course not, I am an elephant. Silly boy."

When the boring antiques show had finally finished the elephant declared,

"I need to take some exercise."

"Exercise?" asked Sam.

"Yes, I need to lose a few pounds. Do you have a bicycle?"

"Yes, but…" spluttered Sam.

"But what?"

demanded the elephant.

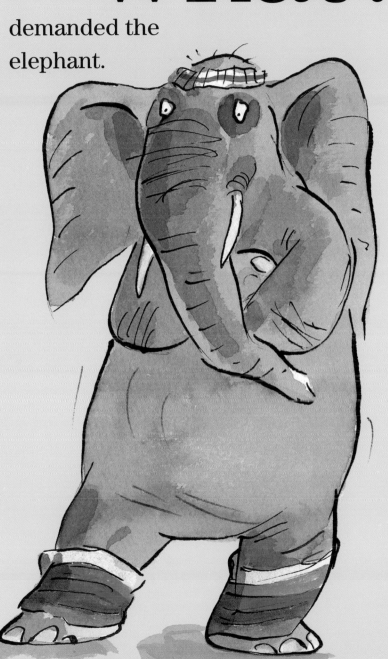

"Well, it's quite small… and… and being an elephant… you might break it."

"How dare you!"

boomed the elephant.

"Now where is it?"

So Sam wheeled his brand-new
bike out of the garage.
"Please be careful,"
he pleaded.

"I know my way
around a bicycle," the elephant said.

"Last year I won the
Tour de France."

The elephant climbed on to the bike.

And as soon as he sat on it…

...he flattened it.

"That bicycle was falling to bits! Silly bits! Silly boy!

"After all that exercise, I need a nap,"
said the elephant. Then he fell asleep in Sam's bed.

Knock, knock, knock. It was the door. Who could it be? Was it his mum back from the shops? Sam hurtled down the stairs to greet her.

But when he opened the door, he couldn't have been more surprised to see…

A massive herd

# of elephants!

"Our friend invited us to stay,"

said the one with the longest trunk.

There were elephants in the kitchen.

Elephants on the stairs.

Even elephants in the downstairs loo.

Meanwhile, Sam rummaged around in his bedroom for the 'Adopt an Elephant' form. When he finally found it he realised something...

He should have read the small print.*

Silly boy.